Take a Streetcar to Meet Your Cat for Supper

Take a Streetcar
to Meet Your Cat
for Supper

by Liana Manukyan Crosby

Illustrations by Jonathan Logsdon

First Printing, 2014

ISBN 978-0-9862620-0-5

www.lianamanukyancrosby.net

For Violet, Jacob, Ramona, and Alexander

Sam loved his mother very much, more than anyone, in fact. But he was also a little afraid of her. Sam knew that one day he would grow up and leave his home and his mother to go seek adventures. All the creatures in the books he read did that. But the thought of leaving, the thought of being alone, frightened him.

Sam also loved his cat, whose name was Silas. Whenever Sam sat down to read a book, Silas would curl up beside him. Sometimes Sam read the book aloud to Silas, and imagined that Silas could understand.

Another thing Sam loved was to ride on streetcars. San Francisco had lots of them, and some of the streetcars were from faraway places like Melbourne, or Milan. He and his mother would stand at the stop and wait for the ding-ding of the bell that the conductor would ring, and Sam would listen for the noise the tracks made, a rumbling and a hissing, as the streetcar approached.

He would climb up the stairs and into the streetcar and run to an empty seat by one of the windows facing the bay. He would catch glimpses of the water as the streetcar moved up or down Church Street. Sometimes, if he was lucky, he would see a sailboat with its white sails stretched out to catch the wind.

It was on the first day of Sam's second grade, on an overcast and rainy day, that a strange and unexpected thing happened. He and his mother stood at the streetcar stop. His mother was holding an umbrella with one hand, Sam's lunch bag in the other, and had her arm around Sam. She was pressing him close to her, to keep Sam sheltered under the umbrella.

4

They waited and waited, and many other people waited too. In a nearby pool of rain water Sam could see the reflection of the dark clouds moving across the sky. All at once, just as he heard the rumbling and hissing of the streetcar tracks, Sam saw a little grey mouse cross the street in a hurry. And then it was gone. People began shuffling and moving toward the approaching streetcar, and all Sam could see were legs and boots and big buttons on dark coats and ladies purses and fingers wrapped around umbrella handles. Sam squeezed his way through the crowd as the crowd pushed and pulled him and carried him up the steps into the streetcar. Once inside, Sam saw one perfect seat ahead, and he ran to claim it.

He sat down, a little damp from the rain, and looked out the window. He was looking for his mother's shape, but couldn't find it.

The doors closed and the streetcar began to move. He looked and looked for his mother, but could not find her.

Sam was frightened. He had no money, and no way of reaching his mother to let her know where he was. The streetcar rattled along the tracks, carrying him farther away. He did not know what to do. So he covered his face with the sleeve of his coat and cried.

When Sam finally stopped his crying and looked up, he saw a very strange scene.

In the middle of the car, standing on top of an ornamented wooden pedestal, was the mouse Sam had seen scurrying across the street.

The mouse had a very loud, deep voice, and was delivering a speech to the people in the car, many of whom had gathered around the pedestal and were listening closely. The people weren't the everyday people Sam had seen when he had first boarded the car. One had the tail of a cat and the beak of a bird. Another looked like a large squirrel but wore pants and a jacket like the ones Sam wore. A third was a sheep with long, drooping ears of a bloodhound, standing on his hind legs and wearing a three-piece suit.

Sam was in such awe that not only did he forget his sadness, but he also did not notice that the car had lifted off its tracks and was flying over the city and snaking through the thick fog toward the clouds.

Somebody in the crowd asked the mouse a question that Sam did not hear. "Trousers with tasseled cuffs, of course," the mouse said as Sam approached the crowd. Through a window Sam could see the thick clouds rushing past.

As Sam stood gaping in wonder, he noticed a creature standing along the fringes of the crowd and wearing a funny-looking tall hat in the shape of a cone. The cone was topped with a small, red pompom. The creature was holding a little notebook and pencil and seemed to be writing down every word the mouse said. From the sides of his hat stuck out the creature's oversized, pointy ears. He also had a nose that seemed inconveniently large for his face. Sam had seen the creature before, but could not remember where. The creature all of a sudden became aware of Sam's presence, and began pushing his way through the crowd until he was standing next to Sam.

"Well?" said the creature, "What do you think?"

"Do I know you?" Sam asked shyly.

"Of course you know me," exclaimed the creature as though it were a silly thing for Sam to ask. "You drew me! And remember how you decided to add this hat at the last minute? It took me some time to forgive you for it. So what do we do?"

"About what?" Sam was confused.

Then all at once he remembered. It was a drawing he had made that his mother had put on the refrigerator door. It was of this creature, and now the creature was real and standing next to him.

"Now that you're here. You shouldn't be here. We must do something."

"Where am I?"

"You're here," said the creature, closing his notebook and tucking it and the pencil carefully into his jacket pocket. "Do you know how you ended up here?"

"No." Sam didn't want to tell this creature that he had been crying.

"Well, there is only one thing to do. You must go to the House."

"Which house?"

"The Yellow House, of course."

"Why?"

"Because he can help you. Now hurry – you must get off here," the creature said as the streetcar came to a stop and its doors opened.

Sam and the creature pushed through the crowd. They leaped out, and Sam's heart skipped a beat. He expected to fall right through the clouds.

But he didn't. The ground below them held them up.

"I've never seen so many strange creatures," said Sam, feeling that it was safe to look around now that there was solid ground under him.

"You mustn't stare," the creature said. "It's not polite. Now go – this road will take you there," he said, pointing ahead. Then he was gone.

Sam hurried along the road until he came to a large yellow building with blue shutters. He stopped at the front door and gazed up at it. It looked inviting and cozy, but also grand.

He knocked on the door. When nobody answered, he tried the knob. The door was unlocked and he cautiously pushed it open and stepped inside.

Sam stood looking down a long hallway. Nobody seemed to be at home; no sound came from anywhere. He was frightened, but also curious.

He walked down the hallway and came to a room with a door that was slightly ajar. Through the opening he could see the light of a fire dancing on the walls. He pushed the door open, and saw a cat, very much like his cat, lounging on a large, comfortable-looking pillow, close to the fire.

The cat opened his eyes a crack and looked at Sam, then licked his nose. "Hi Sam," he said.

As Sam approached the cat, he became more and more convinced that it was his cat. "Silas?" he said.

"Who else?" Silas said as he stood up and stretched, first the front half of his body then the back half. Then he came up to Sam, rubbed his face against the edges of Sam's shoes, and purred. Sam threw his arms around Silas and hugged him, which Silas did not like.

Sam sat in the cozy, fire-lit room, talking to his cat Silas about many things and eating the supper Silas had ordered for them.

While Silas ate an entire roasted chicken (Sam didn't know Silas could eat a whole chicken), and

Sam ate a grilled cheese sandwich (his favorite thing in the world), Sam learned about the adventures Silas had had before he came to live

with Sam. He learned about all the places Silas had seen, and the people he had met. Sam also learned that Silas' favorite book was one Sam had read to him.

"I didn't think you could understand!" Sam said.

Silas said nothing. He was busy cleaning the back of his ear with his paw.

"Where is this place, you know, on the map," Sam asked.

"You know this, Sam," said Silas, licking his paw then rubbing his face with it.

"I do?" Sam thought for a while, munching on a chocolate chip cookie. "I can't think."

"It's all the things you've imagined," said Silas. Sam did not understand.

18

"What was the mouse talking about in the streetcar?"

"Fashion," Silas said. "He advises the creatures on fashion. What with tails and beaks and paws and fur and feathers, it's difficult to know what to wear."

"Are you the only creature here that's just a cat and nothing else?"

"*Just* a cat?" Silas said.

"I didn't mean – "

"I know you didn't, Sam."

Sam and Silas ate until they were very full and talked for a long, long time. Finally, Sam turned to Silas and asked something he had been longing to ask all evening. "Why do you never speak to me when we're at home?"

Silas yawned, stood up, and began walking away, his shoulder blades rising and falling as Sam watched. Sam ran after him.

"Wait!" Sam shouted as he ran out of the room and the house, rushing down the street, following Silas. As he ran faster, so did Silas. It was dark, the fog still lingered, and very soon all Sam could see were small patches of Silas' black and white fur. Other shapes moved past him as he ran, and the fog got thicker.

All of a sudden he felt the ground beneath him jolt, and he stopped. He looked down, and when he looked up again, he was looking out of a streetcar window at one of the churches on Church Street.

He looked around. Everybody was human; no strange creatures, and no Silas.

The streetcar came to a stop. People climbed down the streetcar steps, going about their day in the rain, their umbrellas bobbing up and down as they moved, like cats' tails.

All at once Sam heard his mother's voice calling his name. And very soon after that he was in her arms. After giving Sam many kisses, she began to cry.

"There you are," she said as she sniffled. "I thought I had lost you."

She seemed afraid, so Sam put his arms around her and held her very tight.

Sam made it to school on the first day of his second grade, though a little late. He made new friends that day, and his teacher, who had red hair, read a story to them. In class, he spent his free time drawing yellow houses with blue shutters. There was always a black and white cat looking out of one of the windows.

On his way home from school that day, as he and his mother hurried up their street, Sam looked for the house with the front steps painted to look like the sky, pale blue with clouds swimming along them. On the opposite side of the street he saw his favorite purple house with cactus growing on its walls. He had missed his street.

When they reached their house, Sam ran up the stairs as fast as he could to their front door. He flung the door open and saw his cat sitting on the floor, facing him. Silas stared at Sam, whipped his tail against the floor once or twice, and yawned.

CPSIA information can be obtained at www.ICGtesting.com
Printed in the USA
BVIW12n0106160315
391211BV00002B/3